WHISPER OF THE EAST

TO COMPREHEND THE OTHERNESS OF OTHERS
AS THE ENRICHMENT OF ONE'S OWN BEING;
TO UNDERSTAND ONE ANOTHER,
TO GET TO KNOW ONE ANOTHER,
TO BECOME FAMILIAR WITH ONE ANOTHER,
IS THE FUTURE OF HUMANITY.

ROLF NIEMANN, EDUCATOR, GERMANY

First published in the United States, Great Britain, Canada, Australia, and New Zealand in 2018
by NorthSouth Books, Inc., an imprint of NordSüd Verlag AG, CH-8050 Zürich, Switzerland.

Distributed in the United States by NorthSouth Books, Inc., New York 10016.
Library of Congress Cataloging-in-Publication Data is available.
ISBN: 978-0-7358-4323-3 (trade edition)

1 3 5 7 9 • 10 8 6 4 2

Printed in Latvia by Livonia Print, Riga, 2017.
www.northsouth.com

FRANZISKA MEINERS

WHISPER OF THE EAST

◆ Tales from Arabia ◆

North
South

HELLO AND ASSALAM ALAIKUM.

Welcome to the magical world of Arabia. Can you hear its whisper?

In the olden days, when you wandered through the narrow lanes of Middle Eastern towns, even from a distance you could hear the voices of the *hakawati*, the storytellers. In the early evening they would sit in the coffeehouses telling traditional tales to a crowd of curious onlookers. People were enthralled by the adventures of the heroes, and all they needed was a comfortable seat and attentive ears.

But as time went by, the people scattered and the *hakawati* fell silent. All that remained were the stories. These are a cultural treasure, rich with tradition and filled with bright colors. They were passed on from generation to generation, each one making its own little changes.

That is what happened to the tales in this book. The stories have changed, but the magic remains the same.

Would you like to become part of the story? Then, dear reader, listen carefully, and you will hear about strange and wonderful happenings: the djinn in the bottle, the enchanted prince, and the mysterious dress. Come with me on this journey to distant lands, and get lost in the world of the Arabian fairy tale.

ENJOY LISTENING, READING, AND DISCOVERING!

LEGEND

Words marked with an asterisk (*)
are explained in the glossary.

THE SECRET
OF THE BLACK DRESS

◆◆◆

AN ARABIAN STORY

There was once a king who lived in a rich city. Every day he devoted himself to fulfilling the wishes and needs of his subjects. Many years passed, and the king grew old. And so he sent for his only son, Amir, and said: "I am now an old man. It has become hard for me to go on ruling, my son, and one day you will have to take my place. But first you must find a suitable and clever wife, who will help you to rule."

And so it came to pass that the prince began to search the whole country for a suitable and clever wife. His journey took him to the farthest and strangest places, and he met many women, but he did not fall in love with any of them.

One day he noticed in the distance a large orchard, where ripe fruits shone in the sunlight. When he came closer, he saw between the branches of an orange tree a beautiful peasant girl who was picking the ripe fruit. The way she was standing there— her lovely hair covered by a pretty headscarf, and her cheeks reddened by the hot sun— stirred the prince's heart. He asked her who she was.

She answered: "I'm a peasant girl and I live in this house. This is my garden, and I look after it. And who are you?"

"I'm a traveler and my name is Amir. I'm looking for a girl to marry. Forgive me for being so direct, but I think you would be a suitable bride for me. Will you be my wife?"

The girl stayed silent for a while. Then she answered: "As you can see, I am alone and I must look after all this land and the cattle too. What is your job? Can you work with your bare hands? You don't look like a farmer."

The prince was surprised and answered: "I've never thought about such things."

Then the girl said: "I cannot marry a man who doesn't work and has no ability to do anything."

Then the prince rode back to the palace and told his father about the girl he had met.

"I would like to learn a useful profession, Father," said the prince. "I would like to do some proper work so that this clever peasant girl will agree to marry me."

His father was pleased that the prince wanted to learn a profession, and so he sent for the best weaver in the land to teach his son the art of weaving. The prince learned very quickly, and soon he had made a dress.

The next day he decorated it with colorful cloths and ribbons and took it to give to the peasant girl as a present. She was surprised to see him again, and was very happy that he had taken heed of what she had said. He had understood how important it was to her that the man she married should be able to work.

She put on the dress at once, and when the prince again asked for her hand in marriage, she consented.

There was a great wedding feast at the palace, and there were three days of dancing and laughter. On the fourth day the prince left in order to travel round the land. His wife had suggested this, so that he could get to know his country and his subjects better. He mixed with the people, but was dressed in the clothes of a weaver, which made it easier for them to trust him and talk to him, and also for him to learn from them.

One night, as he was traveling home, the prince was suddenly surrounded by a group of robbers. They threatened him with their sabers and told him to hand over all his money. But Amir had an idea that would save him. Instead of giving them money, he asked their permission to make a dress. Then he suggested they should take the dress to the princess, who would give them as much money as they could wish for.

For five days and five nights the prince sat weaving and sewing. Then he gave the chief of the robbers a long black dress. The chief robber sent one of his men to the palace, and he gave the dress to the princess. When she saw it, she immediately recognized the weaving technique that her husband used. But he had never given her a black dress before. "The color must mean danger," she thought to herself. She took the dress and gave the robber a sackful of coins. As soon as he had left, she ordered her guards to follow him, because he would certainly lead them to the prince.

And that is what happened. The guards followed the man to the robbers' hideout. They overpowered the robbers and freed the prince. Then they took the robbers to the town's prison.

The freed prince returned to the palace and to his princess. They fell into each other's arms, and the prince was thankful that he had such a clever wife. He loved her even more than he had loved her before, because now he knew for certain that he had married the right girl. And they lived happily ever after.

JAMIL AND JAMILA

•

SYRIA

There was once a young girl named Jamila. Her parents had died long ago, and she grew up in her grandparents' house. Their granddaughter meant the world to them, and so they guarded her very carefully. They didn't want her to get foolish ideas like the other children in the village.

The years passed by, and Jamila grew up into a very beautiful and very clever young lady. Her long black hair was smoother and silkier than anyone else's, and her lovely eyes were always sparkling.

She became engaged to a kind and gentle young man named Jamil, and she loved him very much. Soon they would be married.

In Jamila's village there were six other girls her own age. Every time Jamila had to go to the village to get something, she could feel their envious looks stabbing her back. These girls were neither as beautiful nor as clever as Jamila.

The girls came up with a wicked plan to hurt Jamila. They knocked at the grandparents' door and asked if she could go with them to the forest. They said they wanted to gather branches and palm leaves for her wedding. The grandparents consented, and Jamila followed the girls into the forest. She was happy that at last she could spend some time with girls her own age.

When they came to a tall palm tree, one of the girls said: "Look how big and green the palm leaves are right at the top. They would make a wonderful wedding decoration. And over there—can you see those ripe, juicy dates between the leaves." Another girl said: "They look delicious. I wish I could climb up and pick some of them."

The other girls gathered round her and looked longingly up at the tree. Then Jamila said: "I'll climb up there. I have often climbed the palm tree in our garden. I'll pick the dates for you."

Jamila climbed the tree quickly and easily. At last she was able to show the girls that she was not too proud to mix with them, and that she was as brave as they were. She threw some palm leaves and dates down to them, and they eagerly picked them up off the ground. But instead of sharing them equally, they filled their own baskets with the ripe ones, and put the green ones in Jamila's basket.

On the way home, they came to a spring. "This is a wishing spring," said one of the six. "Every girl who closes her eyes, throws her jewelry in it, and makes a wish will live long and will have a happy marriage. We wanted to bring you here, Jamila, so that nothing could stand in the way of your marriage to Jamil."

Jamila smiled with pleasure and said: "How wonderful! Let's all throw our jewelry in there!"

The six of them nodded in agreement and took off their bracelets. And Jamila also took off her precious pendants, rings, and bangles and got ready to throw them all into the deep blue water. But when she closed her eyes to make her wish, the other girls quickly hid their bracelets in their dresses. Instead of their jewelry they threw dates into the water.

They sat for a while on the bank, but then one of the girls said: "I'm tired and hungry. Before we go home, let's eat our dates." And so all the girls reached into their baskets and began to munch their dates.

When Jamila took her own dates out of her basket, she saw that they were hard and unripe. She couldn't understand it, but when she looked round the circle of grinning faces, she realized what the girls had done. She angrily threw her dates at their feet and said: "You've given me all the green dates, although I was the only one who climbed up the palm tree! Why didn't you share them out fairly? In fact I should be the one with the best dates, since I did all the work!"

"But, Jamila," said the others, giggling, "you've got a palm tree in your garden, and we never have the same chance as you to eat such dates."

Jamila jumped up and wanted to go home, but when the other girls also stood up in order to follow her, she heard a loud clinking sound behind her. She turned round and could hardly believe her eyes. One of the girls' bracelets had fallen out of her dress.

And the others were putting their jewelry on. Then Jamila shouted: "You all tricked me! Now all my jewelry is lost forever at the bottom of the spring!"

One of the girls replied spitefully: "Oh, Jamila, forgive us for our little trick. With Jamil as your husband you will soon be so rich that you will have everything you want. But if the jewelry means so much to you, then try to fish it out again. As for us, we're going home."

The girls ran off, giggling. But what they had not told her was that every night a terrible monster came to drink at the spring. Poor Jamila, who did not know about the monster, decided to go back to the spring, in the hope that she might recover her jewelry.

She was still trying to fish it out of the water when night began to fall. The spring was too deep, and now she became afraid, because she had never before been alone in the forest at night.

Suddenly, from behind her she heard a low whispering grew into a deep and terrifying voice. She turned round and gasped with horror. In front of her she saw the biggest and most menacing monster that one could ever imagine. It had teeth like those of a wolf and horns like those of a stag, and yet it moved like a giant slimy toad. It was a **GHOUL***. Its fiery eyes flashed at Jamila as it roared: "Oh, what a pleasant surprise I see before me! Supper served on a silver tray! What are you doing here?"

The trembling Jamila pleaded with him: "Please, dear ghoul, I'll do anything you like, but please, please don't eat me. I dropped my jewelry in the spring and all I want is to get it out again."

The ghoul frowned and said: "Do you want me to get it out for you?"

"Yes, please!" said Jamila. "I daren't go home without it. Everyone will laugh at me when they find out that I let the other girls trick me."

The ghoul looked sharply at her and said: "If I get your precious jewelry for you, then you must do something for me in return. Tomorrow you must come with me to my castle and take my dog for a walk."

Jamila smiled. "Oh, that's not a punishment for me! I'll be happy to do it."

25

And so the ghoul dipped his mouth in the water and with one gulp swallowed the whole spring. Then he reached down for all the precious pieces and put them in Jamila's hands.

"Where do you live?" he asked.

"I live in the next village," answered Jamila, putting her pendants and her bracelets back on again.

"Tomorrow, just before sunset, I shall come on my black stallion to fetch you. So that I know where to find you, hang a white cloth out of your window."

"I'll be waiting for you," said Jamila, and then she ran home.

The next evening, the ghoul arrived at Jamila's house. He was sitting on a beautiful black horse. But when Jamila slipped out of the house—very quietly so that her grandparents wouldn't hear her—she was surprised to see a handsome young man instead of an ugly monster. The young man said: "I am the ghoul's servant, and he sent me to fetch you." Jamila climbed onto the horse, and they rode away.

That evening, Jamil distributed wedding invitations all round the village. When he came to Jamila's house, he saw that she was not there. And she was nowhere to be found during the days that followed. Jamil rode all through the village, asking everyone if they had seen his bride-to-be. But no one had. He became more and more worried, and swore that he would never return until he had found her.

Weeks went by, and Jamil had gone to many villages and towns, and wandered through forests, waded across rivers, and searched the countryside. But nowhere had he found even the slightest clue as to her whereabouts.

After searching for many months, one day Jamil sat down to rest beneath a palm tree. He said to himself: "I can't go on like this. I don't think I shall ever find Jamila. I shall have to give up." He buried his face in his hands and began to weep.

Suddenly, an old woman appeared before him. "Who is Jamila?" she asked. "Why don't you tell me about her?"

"She is a very loving and lovely girl, but she's disappeared," said Jamil. And then he told the old woman all about Jamila and his desperate search for her.

The wise old woman listened patiently, and when he had finished she said: "Exactly a year ago, I saw a girl sitting on the back of a black horse with a handsome young man. They were riding in this direction. I saw a tiny scar on one of her cheeks."

"That must have been her!" cried Jamil, and jumped to his feet. "That was my Jamila!"

"I can see into the very heart of people, and I knew that the man was abducting her. He was only disguised as a young man. In reality he was a ghoul, and ghouls can change into all kinds of things."

The old woman pointed to a distant hill on which stood a castle half hidden in the forest. Then she went on: "Can you see the castle on the hill over there? That is where the ghoul is holding her captive." Jamil nodded. She continued: "Now listen carefully, young man. The ghoul stays awake for seven days and nights, but in three days' time he will begin his sleep, which will last for a month. He has put a curse on Jamila, and she has fallen into a deep sleep. When she wakes up, she will also turn into a ghoul. The only way for you to save her is to cut her long fingernails and her long hair. That will prevent her from changing, and only then will she be freed from the curse. Save her before it's too late."

"But what should I do if the ghoul suddenly wakes up?" asked Jamil.

"When the ghoul sleeps, nothing can wake him," said the old woman, "except the dog that guards him. Only if he hears the dog bark will he wake up. So you must be very careful."

The old woman put her arm round Jamil. "Do not be afraid. I'll give you three magic things to help you on your way."

She opened the bag she was carrying on her back, and gave him a flower from a thorn-bush, a pebble, and a small bottle of clear water.

"If the ghoul follows you, throw this flower in his path. Then throw the pebble, and finally the bottle. Ride as fast as your horse can carry you."

Jamil doubted whether these three tiny things could stop the ghoul, but he trusted the old woman, thanked her, and promised to follow her advice.

Three days later he set off toward the castle on the hill. When he finally reached it, he heard a terrible noise that was louder than a clap of thunder. He remembered the words of the wise old woman. The terrible noise must be the ghoul snoring.

Jamil slipped quietly through the castle gate and began his search, room by room. He walked along endless corridors, and peered into the darkest corners and cellars. And from one room he heard the thunderous snores of the monster. Jamila surely couldn't be far away. He tried each door, but there was only one that opened. Quietly he entered the room, and there he found Jamila. She was lying fast asleep on a bed of stone.

He sat down on the bed and began to cut her long fingernails and her long hair. Suddenly, Jamila opened her eyes, and when she saw him, she sobbed. "Jamil! . . . At last you've come to save me!"

Jamil was so happy to find his beloved safe and sound that he completely forgot about the ghoul's dog. Together they hurried through the long passageways and finally out of the castle gate, where Jamil's horse was waiting. But their footsteps had awakened the dog, and his furious barking awakened the ghoul.

Jamil and Jamila rode as fast as they could and hoped they would get away in time, but when Jamila looked back, she could see the ghoul in the distance and he was gaining on them.

She cried: "Jamil, I can see the ghoul. He's following us and moving very fast!"

Jamil spurred his horse on, but the ghoul was coming ever closer. Then Jamil threw the thorn-bush flower behind them. Immediately, tall and impenetrable thorn-bushes sprang up from the ground. But the thorns could not pierce the leather skin of the ghoul. He simply tore the brambles away with his teeth until he had made a path for himself, and then once more he chased after the pair.

"Can you see anything?" asked Jamil.

Jamila answered: "I can still see him. And he's coming after us at great speed!"

Now Jamil threw the pebble, and a deep chasm opened up behind them, ripping the earth apart and swallowing everything around it. But when the ghoul reached the chasm, he leapt high in the air and turned himself into an eagle. He glided over the split earth, and when he landed on the other side, he turned himself back into a ghoul.

"Is he still following us?" asked Jamil, and again Jamila looked fearfully behind her. "Yes, he's catching up! Ride like the wind!"

Jamil opened the little bottle and shook the water out. A great sea surged up behind them, and even the ghoul could not cross it. So when he reached its shore, he said to himself: "If I can't cross the water, I shall drink it all, right down to the last drop."

Just as he had done with the spring, he dipped his lips into the water and started to drink. He drank and he drank, and the higher and stronger the waves, the bigger grew his belly.

Then suddenly there was a loud explosion and . . . *fffttt* . . . the ghoul had simply burst.

Jamil and Jamila reached home safely. When they told everyone what the mean girls had done to Jamila, all six were banished to another village. Their inner ugliness then made its way to their outside, and they became old and ugly.

But Jamil and Jamila got married and lived happily ever after.

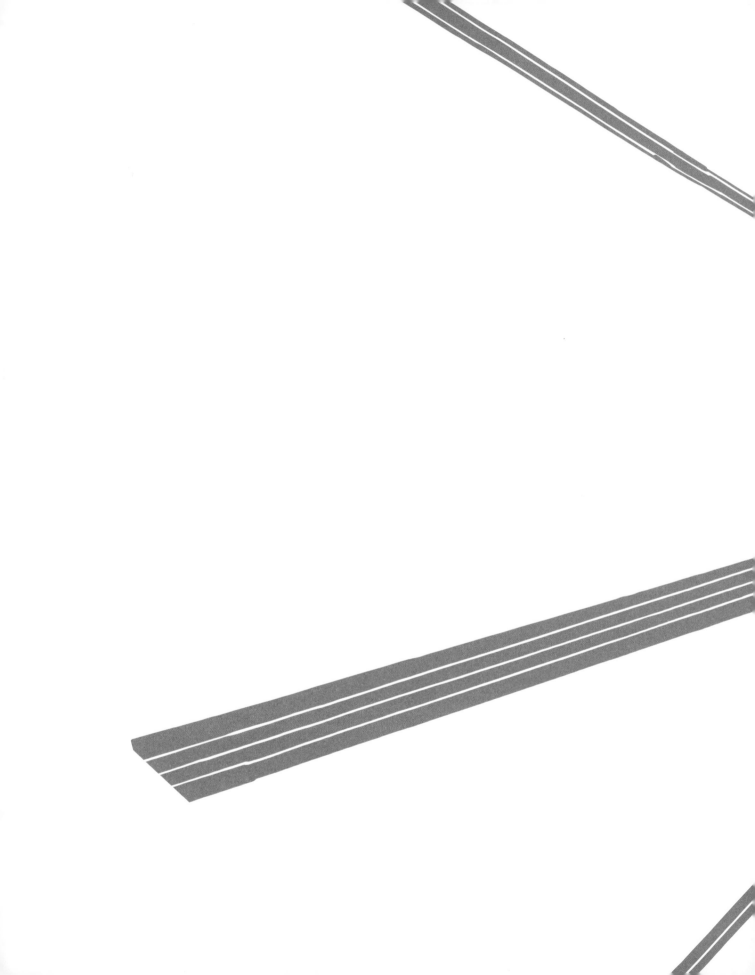

THE FISHERMAN AND THE DJINN

◆◆

ADAPTED FROM »A THOUSAND AND ONE NIGHTS«

In Beirut, people used to tell the story of an old fisherman who lived with his family in a little hut on the seashore just outside the city. Every day for forty years the fisherman had thrown his net into the sea. He always hoped to make a big catch with which to feed his family, but for several weeks he had not had much luck. Once more he waded out into the water and cast his net, and in his despair he thought to himself: "Fortune does not seem to favor me. So why should I expect to get a good catch today?"

He waited for a long time but nothing happened. He was just about to give up and pull in his net when he noticed that something was holding it back. He made a great effort and dug his feet into the sand, but when at last he succeeded in dragging the net to the shore, he was more than a little disappointed. There were no fish in his net, or even any edible shellfish. The only thing he had caught was a dead donkey. Sadly, he freed the dead animal from his net and let it lie on the wet sand.

Then he carefully patched his net, took it far out, and threw it even farther into the ocean. He had not been waiting long when once more he felt a powerful tug at the net. Full of hope, he again dragged the net to the shore, but this time found himself looking at a huge bucket that was full of holes and glass splinters, algae, and stones. Tears came to his eyes, because once again he was afraid that he would have to go home empty-handed. But when he turned around and saw in the distance the house of all his loved ones, he made himself go on. He must try his luck for the third and last time.

He threw his net out, watched as the waves swallowed it up, and waited. Almost an hour went by, and then suddenly there was a violent jerk as the net was pulled deeper down. "This must be a huge catch," he said to himself, and was already starting to dream of his daughters' faces when he brought home a real feast. He gathered all his strength. Panting and red-faced he heaved the net out of the water and spread it out on the shore.

Yet again there were no fish in the net. To his great disappointment, all he had caught was an earthenware jug with a closed leaden lid. He shook the jug to and fro, but there was no sound from inside. "There must be something in it," he said. "It's far too heavy to be empty." He took out his fisherman's knife, levered the lid off, and

looked inside the jug. But he still couldn't see anything. It appeared to be empty. Disappointed yet again, he was just about to throw it back into the sea when suddenly a thick, dark cloud of smoke rose up from inside. The smoke enveloped the fisherman and he could not even see his hand in front of his eyes. Then gradually the smoke took the shape of a figure that grew bigger and bigger. It was the largest and most terrifying

being he had ever seen. It was a demon **DJINN***. Its head towered thirteen feet up into the sky, and from there it glared down at the fisherman with its great glowing eyes. Its mouth was like a big black cave; its teeth were like the sharp points of spears; its shoulders were as broad as a castle gate, and its hands were like metal shields.

The djinn bent down toward the trembling fisherman, and spoke in a deep rumbling voice: "Listen well, old man! Today is the day when you must die. I have sworn an oath that I will take my revenge on whoever frees me from this jug, and I will kill him!"

The frightened fisherman asked: "Why are you talking of revenge? I have done you a favor by freeing you from the jug, so why do you want to kill me?"

The djinn answered: "Six hundred years ago I rebelled against the King of the Djinns. As a punishment he imprisoned me in this jug and had me thrown into the sea. For the first two hundred years I swore that whoever freed me would be showered with gifts and I would make him king. But no one freed me. After another two hundred years in this prison I swore that I would serve my liberator forever and make all his wishes come true. But again no one helped me. And so I became angry, and determined that I would punish and kill whoever freed me, to spite the King of the Djinns for one last time—because he would not be pleased if his orders from the Underworld cost the life of a human. That would make him into a bad ruler. Now you can choose how you want to die."

The fisherman stood rooted to the spot, and knew that soon he would die. Sadly he thought of his family, who would now be left fatherless. And that made him very angry at the djinn, who had so arrogantly given himself the right to take someone's life. He looked once more at the jug, and suddenly he had an idea. He said: "Dear Djinn, what you say is very moving, but I don't quite believe you. Look at yourself. Huge as you are, you could never have fitted into this jug. Not even one of your hands would fit in. I don't think it was me that freed you, because I don't think you were ever in the jug!"

"What do you mean?" asked the djinn, raising his voice. "How dare you question the truth of my story! It is the nature of a djinn always to tell the truth. For this insult I shall kill you at once."

The brave fisherman defied him once again: "I am not afraid of you. You are a liar, and you never fitted into this jug!"

Fuming with rage, the djinn towered up even higher toward the sky. "You have sealed your fate, old man. I shall show you that you are wrong, and then I shall throw you to the sharks so they can eat you." Higher and higher he soared, until he had transformed himself into a dark whirlwind of dust and smoke. And faster and faster he twisted himself into a spiral before plunging down in a gust of wind, deeper and deeper into the jug. "You see! I spoke the truth!" he squeaked from the very depths.

"Yes, I see!" cried the fisherman, and joyfully he seized hold of the jug and slammed the lid down over the opening.

Only then did the djinn realize that the fisherman had outwitted him. With a whine and a whimper he called out: "No, no! You tricked me! Please let me out again. I promise that I will give you all the treasures in the world and then never trouble you again, or harm you or kill you."

The fisherman answered: "Let me tell you, dear Djinn, I don't need all the treasures in the world. All I need is a good catch with which to feed my family. That was the reason why I threw my net into the water, and why I shall go on throwing my net day after day. Because no rich gifts could please me as much as having a healthy, happy family." With these words he walked out into the water and threw the jug back into the surging sea, where it sank down to the seabed with the djinn locked inside.

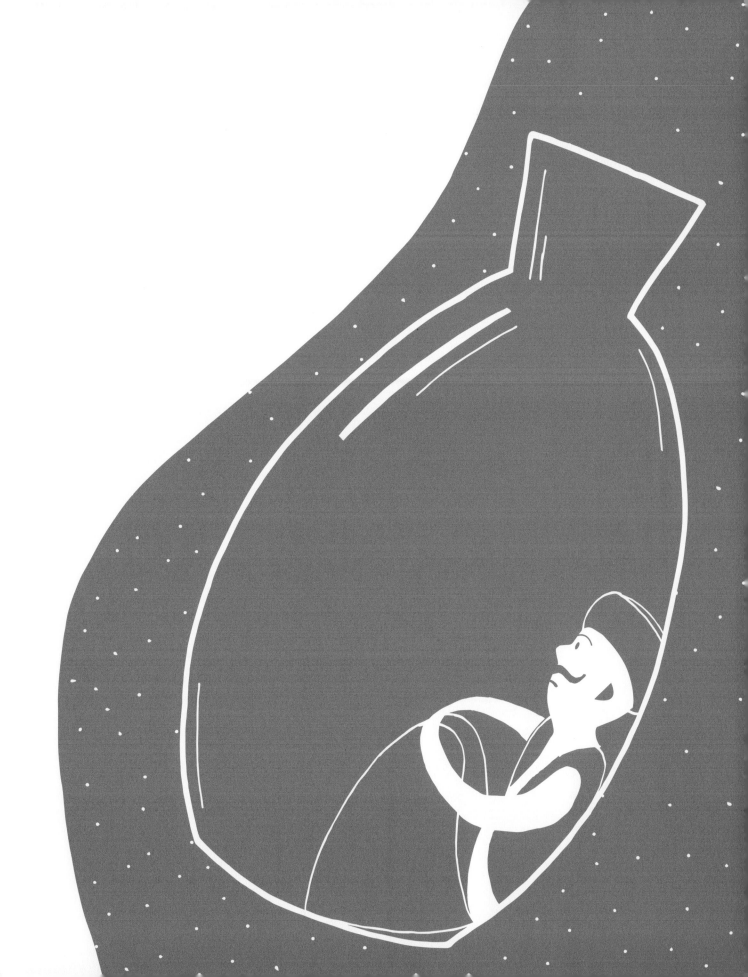

With renewed hope and courage, he picked up all his things from the shore and for the last time that day cast his net. He waited for some time on the sand, and had dozed off when suddenly he was awoken by a powerful tug on the string of his net. Once again, filled with expectations, he heaved the heavy net back to the shore, and then he rubbed his eyes in disbelief. He had caught the biggest catch of his entire life: large fish, small fish, shellfish of all kinds now lay in a huge pile by the water's edge. And among them the fisherman found something else. It was a small glass bottle in which there was a rolled-up piece of paper. Full of curiosity he opened the bottle and unrolled the paper. On it, in handwriting, was the following message:

DEAR FISHERMAN,

THANK YOU FOR REMAINING FAITHFUL TO MY ORDERS AND SENDING THAT
REBELLIOUS DJINN BACK INTO THE SEA. YOU HAVE SAVED MY HONOR.

YOUR HUMBLE DEED DESERVES TO BE REWARDED.
I HOPE YOU WILL MAKE YOUR FAMILY HAPPY WITH THIS CATCH.

KING OF THE DJINNS

And so, overjoyed, the fisherman picked up his catch and set out for home. When he turned round once more to look at the shore, he saw the sea shining on the horizon. And the dead donkey had come back to life and galloped away in the moonlight.

THE LITTLE CAMEL

♦

PALESTINE

KING,
BE KIND TO YOUR SLAVES
AND BEWARE OF THE DEVIL'S PUNISHMENTS.

There was once a woman who did not have much money. The fact that she was poor was of little concern to her. What she really longed for was to have a child. Day after day she would go to the marketplace, where there would be children playing all around her, and she would watch them with an aching heart. Many years passed, and still the poor woman was childless.

One night she went out walking beneath the starlit sky. The village had long since gone to bed, and there was no sound except the snorting of a nearby camel that was resting with its calf. The woman sadly took off her headscarf, looked up at the stars, and prayed to God to let her have a child. "I've waited patiently for so long. But even this mother camel can consider herself happier than me. There is nothing I want more than a child to which I can give all my love. Let it be human or animal, it will be mine and that is all that matters."

After a few days, the woman felt something moving in her stomach. Full of joy, she jumped up and cried: "God the Merciful has heard my prayer! I'm pregnant!"

The first few months went by, and the woman could not have been happier. As time passed, she noticed that her stomach was growing much faster and much bigger than the stomachs of other pregnant women, but she thought nothing of it. At the end of nine months, and a long night of labor, she finally gave birth. What she held in her arms, however, was not an outsize baby human. Almost unbelievably, it was a baby camel.

All at once a large crowd of people gathered around her. Her neighbors made horrible faces, slapped their heads with their hands, and rolled their eyes. No one could believe what they saw. But the poor woman was overjoyed and called her son Djadi.

During the day Djadi grazed in the fields with the sheep, and at night he sheltered with them in their pen behind the house.

When Djadi was full grown, he came to his mother and said: "Mother, I would like to have a wife." And so his mother set out to find a suitable bride for her son. The search was more difficult than she had expected. No father was willing to give his daughter's hand in marriage to a camel. When the mother came home without a bride-to-be, her son said: "I didn't want to marry any of those girls. I want the SULTAN'S* youngest daughter to be my wife."

The poor mother knew that the Sultan's youngest daughter, Princess Mayla, was the most beautiful of all his daughters, and the Sultan loved her more than life itself. But although she was afraid to ask him for his most beautiful daughter's hand without being able to offer him anything in return, she summoned up all her courage and asked for an audience with him. Her request was granted, and in due course she humbly knelt before him in the middle of the Great Hall. In a gentle voice he asked her: "Tell me what it is that you wish for." He had a kind heart, and always talked respectfully to everyone.

"I have come on behalf of my son to make a request to Princess Mayla. My son would like to marry her," said the woman.

"Tell me about your son," replied the Sultan.

"He is my pride and joy, but he was born a camel."

The Sultan smiled into his long gray beard, but he did not want to make the woman look foolish in front of all the courtiers, and so he said: "Your son should be given the same chance as all the others who ask for the hand of my beloved Mayla. People say that her beauty is like the light of a thousand stars. So bring me a thousand gold coins as bride money, and your son shall have my daughter."

When the mother returned home, she scolded her son. "Tell me, how do you think we can ever earn the bride money? We do not even have one single gold coin! Now you will never get a wife."

Djadi remained quite calm and answered: "I know a way. But you must trust me. Go back to the palace and ask the Sultan to send his soldiers outside the city. They should take some large empty sacks with them, and strong horses."

His mother had no idea what her son was planning, but she did as he asked.

The next day, all the soldiers and their horses assembled outside the city gates. They looked at one another and frowned, and it was obvious from the expression on their faces that they were wondering what they were doing there.

Djadi had been waiting for them by the city wall, and now he led them to a large, gnarled tree. He stamped three times with his hoofs, and a huge dark hole opened up in the ground before them. It was the entrance to a long underground tunnel. Once again Djadi led the way, and one by one the soldiers followed him into the darkness. The tunnel led to a big underground cave. When the soldiers looked around the cave, they saw mountains of shining gold and jewels. They squinted their eyes, blinded by all these precious things, and they could scarcely believe what they saw.

They filled their sacks, loaded the horses, and rode out through the tunnel. When Djadi also emerged into the daylight, once more he stamped three times and the earth closed up beneath them.

Then Djadi himself went to the Sultan's palace. He stepped before the Sultan in the Great Hall, and said: "I have brought you far more than you asked for. And now you must keep your side of the agreement."

The Sultan turned pale when he saw the pile of gold coins and other treasures. How could he have imagined that a poor woman's son—who was also a camel—would bring him what he had asked for, and more besides? But he had given his word, and his word was sacred. The Sultan called for the KADI*—the wisest of judges—who could find no solution to the problem, and so the Sultan had to tell his daughter about the calamity. Mayla wept bitter tears, but she could not disobey the commandments of her father.

HAVE NO FEAR!

And so that evening, in a great procession that was more like a funeral than a celebration, the princess, surrounded by her guards, was taken to Djadi's house. There, cowering with fear, she waited for her future husband. When the door opened, she looked up, and was astonished. In front of her stood a tall and handsome young man, who gazed at her with the gentlest of eyes.

He spoke in a soft voice: "Do not be afraid, Mayla. I am your husband, Djadi. I am the son of the King of the Djinns, but an evil djinn put a curse on me, and I was trapped in the body of a camel. Only by marrying you could I be changed back. But sadly, I can only resume my human form at night. I promise that I will come to you every night if you give me your word that you will keep my secret to yourself. If you break your promise, I shall disappear forever."

Some weeks went by, and then the soldiers from a neighboring land marched on the Sultan's city. With heavy heart, the Sultan prepared for war. When Princess Mayla told Djadi about her father's problem, he said without a moment's hesitation: "When the enemy soldiers advance, I shall fight. I shall wear white clothing, and I shall ride a mighty horse. But you must not tell anyone that it's me!"

In the twilight, all the people climbed onto their roofs to watch the battle going on in the starlit streets. Mayla also watched tensely with some other women. They all tried to outdo one another in praising the bravery of their menfolk. One said: "Look, there's my husband! He knocked the enemy down with one hand!" Another said: "My husband is at the front there. The Sultan has already given him a medal of honor."

While the women carried on with their loud dispute over whose husband was the bravest, Princess Mayla kept looking out for Djadi. She found it hard not to join in the conversation, and waited nervously for her husband to ride into battle and help her father.

Suddenly, a knight in white robes galloped onto the battlefield. He swung his sword to the left and the right, and killed seven men with a single blow. All the women fell silent, and then began to murmur quietly among themselves. Speculation grew as to whose husband might be hiding behind the flowing white robes.

While the women had been praising their husbands, Princess Mayla had tried hard not to listen, so that she would not be tempted to speak. But her heart was now bursting with pride. Before she could stop herself, she cried: "Djadi! The knight is my husband, Djadi!" Then at once she slapped her hand over her mouth. The women around her gazed at her in surprise. Only she knew what. She had broken his commandment.

The city celebrated the Sultan's victory all through the night, but Princess Mayla waited in vain for her husband to return. By morning she could bear it no longer. She hurried out of the house to search for him, but although she ran through every street, searched behind every wall and every tree, Djadi had disappeared without a trace.

Months went by, and still there was no sign of her husband. Sick with worry, she had now been lying in bed for weeks, unable even to stand. Her father was deeply concerned about his daughter's health, and felt partly responsible for her condition. After all, it was he who had made her marry Djadi. He tried to think of ways to make his daughter happy again. He ordered his finest architect to build an especially beautiful **HAMMAM***, which was decorated with gold and marble. Then he invited every woman in the country to come to this bath-house, but as payment they must tell the princess a story.

Ladies from all over the land prepared to go and bathe in the royal hammam. But many came only in order to catch a glimpse of the princess, or to tell her about their handsome, bride-seeking sons.

In a village out in the desert there lived an old widow who owned little more than the clothes she was wearing and who had never bathed in a hammam. She summoned up all her courage and decided to accept the Sultan's invitation. Although she had no good stories to tell the princess, she hoped she might think of something on the way. She asked her grandson to accompany her, and the two of them set off on the long journey over the hills and down through the valleys.

In the desert, night falls very quickly. When they had reached about halfway to the palace, they rested at a small oasis, and to protect themselves against the dangers of the desert, they climbed into an acacia tree.

While they were sitting there, they heard a sudden rustling sound among the leaves. A hen and a cock had sat down on one of the branches and were clucking away to each other. The cock croaked: "Oh, Waters of Heaven, rain down upon us!" And the hen cackled: "Oh, Grandfather Wind, blow your great gusts!" At once there was a mighty storm and the rain drummed down from the sky.

When the storm finally faded away, the woman and her grandson—now soaking wet and battered by the wind—saw an astonishing sight. Where the last drops of rain had fallen to the earth in front of the acacia tree, the ground suddenly opened up, and one by one a line of men climbed out of the Underworld. On their strong shoulders they carried tables, chairs, and the finest dishes, plates, and cups.

They were all decorated with gold, and little gems had been worked into some of the wood. The men covered the tables with delicious exotic foods, poured out the finest wines, and then disappeared again into the earth. Next, a flock of white doves flew high into the air before settling down on the tables and the ground. They pecked here and there, and splashed in the puddles.

After this, there was a loud sound of cooing and all at once the doves turned into attractive men and women. Each of them sat down at a table, and then they seemed to wait. The woman and her grandson could see that there were exactly forty of them, because there were no unoccupied tables. One especially young woman obviously got tired of waiting, and timidly put out her hand to pick up a date. Immediately her neighbor stopped her and said:

"YOU MUSTN'T DO IT. THAT'S A SIN!
ONLY THE MASTER CAN BEGIN!"

The old widow and her grandson wondered who the "master" might be. Now a bright light shone out of the earth and lit up the whole tree. A tall young man of indescribable beauty stepped forth. He sat down on a large silk cushion, took a sip of tea, and nodded to each of the young ladies in turn, though he somehow seemed to be deep in thought. The nod must have been the sign for all of them to start eating. And so the feast began, but everyone ate alone and in silence. The only sound was an occasional sigh from the young man. The old woman in the acacia tree even thought she could see a few teardrops running down his cheeks.

When all the diners had eaten their fill, the young man reached out for an apple, which he cut into four pieces. Then he said:

"ONE PART I GIVE TO THE EAST,
ONE PART I GIVE TO THE WEST,
ONE PART FOR ME AT MY FEAST,
AND ONE FOR THE GIRL I LOVE BEST."

Then he stamped on the ground, and a shaft opened up into which all the tables, chairs, and dishes disappeared, together with the girls and, finally, himself.

When dawn broke, the old woman and her grandson climbed down from the acacia tree. Still shaken by the events they had witnessed that night, they set out again on their journey.

When they entered the palace, they were taken through long passageways until they reached a door. There they had to wait until a guard signaled to them to enter. Inside the room Princess Mayla lay upon seven mattresses and under seven blankets.

The old woman spoke: "Your Highness, I came here without knowing anything that would make a good story. But during the journey I had an experience that was like a dream. And yet it was real. I saw a sight so magical and yet so sad that I can scarcely believe it myself. I have never seen a young man of such pure beauty . . ."

The princess lay quite still, but listening. In a weak voice she said: "Tell me the whole story. Who was the young man you speak of?"

Then the old widow told her the story of how she had set out on her journey, had climbed a tree, and had seen everything from above. The more she talked, the more attentive the princess became. One by one, she threw off her blankets. And when the old woman said: "Finally, a wondrously handsome young man emerged, with large shining eyes . . ." the princess sat up as straight as a candle on her seven mattresses. The old woman described how the young man had cut an apple into quarters and had spoken a verse:

"ONE PART I GIVE TO THE EAST,
ONE PART I GIVE TO THE WEST,
ONE PART FOR ME AT MY FEAST,
AND ONE FOR THE GIRL I LOVE BEST."

The princess leapt from her bed and asked the old woman to take her to the acacia tree.

For six nights the princess watched and waited up in the branches, but nothing happened. Could it really be true that the handsome young man was her missing Djadi?

By the seventh night she had almost given up hope. Then suddenly a cock and a hen settled on one of the branches. They clucked away to each other: "Oh, Waters of Heaven, rain down upon us!" said the cock. And the hen cackled: "Oh, Grandfather Wind, blow your great gusts!" Then a mighty storm broke above them, and the wind howled and the rain drummed.

When the storm faded away, everything happened just as the old woman had described. The white doves flew up and changed into young women, and the young man came and sat in their midst. The princess could scarcely believe her eyes, but her heart leapt with joy. He was indeed her husband, Djadi. Then she watched as he stamped on the ground, and the shaft opened up into which the furniture and the guests all disappeared.

The princess swiftly climbed down the tree, and just before the ground closed up again, she squeezed through the crack.

Mayla followed her husband deep into the earth, until at last she caught up with him. She touched him on the shoulder, and when he turned around, the sight of her made him gasp. She flung her arms round his neck and cried: "Come back to your wife, who was sick with worry for you!"

Then Djadi said: "At last you have found me! I was also in the depths of despair here in the Land of the Djinns. I was held captive after you broke my commandment. But you have righted your wrong by following me to the Land of the Djinns. Out of love for me, you have crossed the border between the world above and the world below, and so you have lifted the curse on me and I can go home. And I shall never have to change into a camel again. From now on, I can live by your side as your husband."

THEIR HAPPINESS WAS BOUNDLESS AND COULD NEVER FADE AWAY,
FOR THEY HAD LEARNED AS YOU WILL LEARN: TRUE LOVE WILL FIND A WAY.

THE OLD PAIR OF SHOES

◆◆

A TALE FROM ARABIA

There was once a merchant who lived in Baghdad and whose name was Abu Karim. He was a very rich man and was well known throughout the city.

None of the other merchants liked him, because every day he would go to the **BAZAAR*** on the hunt for bargains. He would haggle with the spice seller, the carpet seller, and the perfume seller. Then he would take the spices, carpets, and perfumes, and the oil of roses, scarves, and shawls to the next bazaar and sell the same goods for four times as much as he had paid.

That was why Abu Karim was well known—not for his wealth but for his mean and miserly behavior. He would never even spend his money, either on himself or—least of all—on helping others.

The proof of this lay in his shoes. For years he had worn the same pair of shoes, and by now they were tattered and full of holes. But he refused to buy a new pair. When he came to the bazaar in his worn-out shoes, everyone mocked him, but he would simply shake his head and resolve to go on wearing them until they fell apart.

One day, after a particularly busy time in the bazaar, Abu Karim went to take a bath in the *hammam*. When he had finished bathing, he suddenly realized that his shoes had disappeared. In the place where his old ones had been, there now stood a brand-new pair, all shining and beautifully crafted. Some children had played a joke on him and had secretly exchanged the shoes.

Abu Karim, however, was delighted to be given a free pair of shoes, and he said: "Ah, once more Fortune is on my side." With these words he slipped his feet into the new shoes and happily made his way home.

A few minutes later, the most famous judge in Baghdad climbed out of his bath and discovered to his disgust that his shoes had disappeared, and in their place was an old pair that was full of holes. "Someone has stolen my shoes!" shouted the *kadi* in a voice that echoed all through the *hammam*. At once a group of bathers gathered around him as he stood there in despair holding the tattered shoes in his hands. They all knew at once who the old shoes belonged to, and so the rumor quickly spread that Abu Karim must have stolen the judge's shoes.

The *kadi* therefore sent his men to arrest Abu Karim and bring him before the court. When he entered the courtroom, everybody started to laugh, because they could all see the proof of his guilt on his feet—the judge's beautiful shoes. The *kadi* did not need long to pronounce his judgment, and duly imposed a very large fine on the merchant.

Abu Karim was furious. He stormed home, now wearing his old tattered shoes, and he cursed them: "You have brought me bad luck!" he raged. "Because of you I have lost all that hard-earned money. The time has come for me to get rid of you once and for all." So saying, he went to the bank of the river and hurled his old shoes into the fast-flowing waters. They were quickly carried downstream, and soon they were no more to be seen.

A few days later, there was a knock on the merchant's door. When he opened it, he found himself confronted by two angry fishermen. "When we took in our nets this morning, all we found were these old shoes, and they had torn holes in our nets! Not a single fish was left for us to sell! And they're your shoes, aren't they?" The merchant could scarcely believe his eyes when the fishermen waved his old shoes in front of his nose. "And now you owe us money for the damage your shoes have done!"

Embarrassed and angry, Abu Karim took the shoes from them and gave the fishermen a large bag of coins. When he had closed his door, he hurled the shoes onto the floor and stamped all over them. "You—bring—me—nothing—but—bad—luck!" he roared. "Now I shall bury you once and for all!"

He stormed outside and began to dig a hole in his garden. Suddenly, his spade hit something hard in the ground. When he looked more closely, a great fountain of water splashed up into his face. He had hit a water pipe. Within minutes he was surrounded by a crowd of angry neighbors. They no longer had any running water. And so once again Abu Karim was arrested and taken before the court.

This time the *kadi* was even more annoyed. "I am going to double your fine! Your shoes have brought nothing but bad luck to our whole community. Look how many people have suffered because of you!"

Now more than ever, Abu Karim was determined to get rid of his accursed shoes. He decided to burn them, but as they were still wet, he put them outside on his balcony to dry.

A dog spotted the shoes from a distance, and climbed onto a rock beside the balcony. Then he leaned over and began to play with the shoes. It did not take long before they fell off the balcony, and they did so at precisely the moment when a camel driver was taking his herd underneath. As luck would have it, the shoes landed right on the head of one of the camels. It was so startled that it panicked and ran away, taking three other camels with it. The animals disappeared in the winding alleyways of the city, and the camel driver was left loudly cursing his fate and trying to calm his two remaining camels. Then he picked up the old shoes from the street, looked up at the balcony, and shouted: "Abu Karim, you'll pay for this! Thanks to you and your shoes I've lost four camels! I'll never earn enough to live on with the two camels that are left. And it's all your fault!"

The camel driver reported what had happened to the authorities, and once more Abu Karim was summoned before the court. The kadi glared at the merchant. "You have caused much suffering to many people with your shoes. Now you must pay the full price, and you will look after the camel-owner until he is able to earn a living for himself and buy new camels."

Abu Karim wept bitter tears. He could see himself now on the verge of poverty. Bent and bowed, he dragged himself homeward. At the side of the road he encountered an old, barefoot beggar.

"Why are you so miserable?" asked the beggar.

"Because of these shoes," said Abu Karim, "I have lost all my money and all my friends. If I hadn't been so mean and had bought myself new shoes earlier, none of this would have happened."

The beggar said: "I would give a lot just to have any shoes at all. But if I had as much money as you, I would be able to buy shoes for all my friends as well."

His words made Abu Karim think. He had quite forgotten that there were such poor people in the city who had no shoes at all.

Then he said to the beggar: "These shoes are really too old for anyone to wear. But I promise you, tomorrow I will go to the bazaar and buy a new pair of shoes for myself and for you as well. And I shall put these old shoes in the rubbish and be rid of them once and for all!"

The beggar smiled from ear to ear and hurried away to tell his friends about his unexpected good fortune.

And so it came to pass that Abu Karim changed his way of life. He no longer hoarded his wealth, and he no longer kept his shoes until they were too tattered to wear.

On the contrary, he became wonderfully generous with the money he earned. He not only bought new shoes for himself every year, but he also bought new shoes for everyone who could not afford to buy their own.

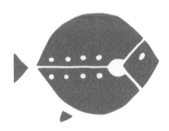

THE FISHERMAN AND THE MERMAID

• • •

A TALE FROM ARABIA

There was once a father who lived in a modest little house with his three children. The month of **RAMADAN*** was nearing its end, and soon they would celebrate the end of the fast. The children had been looking forward to the festival for a long time, and they asked their father what presents he would give them. "I would like a beautiful pair of shoes," said Aicha. Fatma said: "I would like a new shawl." Hana, the youngest of the three, wanted a big pot full of sweets. She had had to do without sweets all through the month.

When the father saw how excited his children were, he felt very sad. He was a fisherman, and recently his catch had been very small. How could he get enough money to make his children's wishes come true?

At daybreak the fisherman sat in his boat and rowed out to sea. He could think more clearly there. As usual he threw out his net and thoughtfully sat gazing at the waters. After a while, he saw something shining in his net. "Maybe it's the scales of a big fish shining in the sunlight," he said to himself. He pulled the net out of the water, but what he had thought were the scales of a fish turned out to be a large glass bottle. In his disappointment, he let the bottle slip out of his hand and roll to the other side of the boat.

Suddenly, there was a deep rumbling sound, and out of the bottle rose a thick cloud of white smoke. Before the fisherman could even move, a giant was standing before him, trying to find something to hold onto in the little boat. The fisherman stared at him wide-eyed, but the giant looked so gentle, and was having such trouble fitting into the boat, that the fisherman was not in the least afraid. In a soft, deep voice the giant said with a smile: "I see you're not frightened of me, my dear fisherman. How nice to see! Thank you for rescuing me from my thousand years in captivity! That bottle was extremely tight! Now I owe you a wish of your choosing, so what will it be?"

The fisherman said: "There is something I really would like—a mermaid who will give me a lock of her golden hair. Then I could sell it for a lot of money. My wish is to meet a MERMAID*."

The giant replied: "Nothing could be simpler. I'll take you to the golden grotto where the mermaids live. As a giant I can fly across all the countries and all the seas in the world, so climb on my back and I'll carry you over the highest mountains and the deepest valleys. But the last stage of our journey will take us deep down into the ocean before we finally reach the grotto."

The fisherman rowed back to the shore, and then climbed onto the broad back of the giant. With a powerful push, the giant thrust himself up from the ground and flew high into the sky. On their journey over the ocean the fisherman saw all kinds of sea creatures that he had never seen before: brightly colored fish that glided in shoals through the water, dolphins, sharks, and turtles. Once he could feel his fingers itching and he was about to reach out toward the fish when a gust of wind almost blew him off the giant's back. After that he held on very tightly, and onward they went. From above he could see huge whales slowly pushing through the waves. Then the giant began to descend lower and lower over the sea until the fisherman could almost dip his feet into the water.

"Hold tight!" the giant shouted to his rider, and they plunged down into the blue waters. As they dived deeper and deeper, they passed beautiful coral reefs out of which peeped the shiniest fish, deep-sea shrimps, and sea horses. Suddenly, an octopus wound its long tentacles round one of the fisherman's legs, but the giant cleverly twisted and turned until the octopus let go of its victim.

Slowly they drifted upward again toward the surface of the water, and the fisherman looked up. The sunlight reflected in the water almost blinded him, but as they moved on, he realized that it wasn't the sunlight's reflection at all. It was the dazzling golden walls of a cave. The giant and his rider emerged right in the middle of it. "This is the Grotto of the Mermaids," said the giant. "I shall go and sit on a rock over there, and you can wait here. Your presence alone will attract the mermaids."

The fisherman also sat on a rock and waited. He had not been there long when a creature came out of the water, and he had never seen anyone so beautiful. It was a girl whose hair shimmered in the magic light of the grotto and whose legs had been replaced by a tail full of indescribable colors. Her ice blue eyes gazed curiously at the fisherman, and her golden hair swung gently to and fro in rhythm with the waves.

The fisherman was overwhelmed by the sight of her. Then his eyes fell on her wonderful hair. He swiftly grasped a strand and held it tightly in his hand. The mermaid froze with terror. "What are you doing?" she whimpered.

"Don't be afraid," said the fisherman. "I made a wish to come here so that I could ask you for a lock of your golden hair. I would like to exchange it for presents that I can give to my children."

Then the mermaid said: "Please let go of my hair. I cannot give you a lock of it, dear fisherman. My hair holds the secret of my being. A mermaid's hair must never be cut, because otherwise she will lose her tail and die."

Deeply disappointed, the fisherman let the strand of hair slide back into the water. Now he had used up the one wish granted to him by the giant, and he would return home empty-handed.

As he sat there so sadly, head in his hands, more and more mermaids gathered round him. When they saw how desperate he was, they all looked at one another. At last the eldest spoke: "Do not be sad, fisherman. All is not lost. We are grateful to you for sparing our sister, and you should be rewarded. We cannot give you any of our golden tresses, but we are willing to give you one of our scales. Go back home now, and on the morning of the feast, when you break your fast, look very carefully into your fishing net."

The giant and the fisherman returned to land, and the giant bade the fisherman a gentle farewell before disappearing just as he had appeared, in a cloud of white smoke.

On the morning of the feast, as the first ray of sunshine lit up the sky, the fisherman rowed out to sea as usual and scanned the waves. After a while, he pulled his net back in, and what he saw was so amazing that his face broke into the broadest of smiles. As had been promised, between two large fish he found a single golden scale. In his delight, he leapt to his feet and did a dance of joy. Then he turned, looked out to sea, and bowed to show his gratitude for this precious gift.

He returned home to celebrate the Festival of the Breaking of the Fast, and for the first time to give his children the wonderful presents they had wanted. The sale of the golden scale in fact brought him far more money than he had expected. He was even able to put a part of it to one side so that he could pay for his whole family's schooling, clothes, and food.

From that time onward, whenever he rowed out to sea and watched the sunlight dancing on the waves, he was sure it was a mermaid whose golden hair and scales were shining under the water.

BAZAAR

The word comes from the Persian *bazar* and means a market. In the East this takes the form of narrow lanes of shops in which one can buy a large variety of wares (shoes, carpets, lamps, etc.).

DJINN

A mostly invisible creature that God created out of fire. *Djinns* can be good or evil, and can appear to people in many different forms.

GHOUL

A monster of the desert that lies in wait for lost travelers so that he can abduct them. *Ghouls* eat people and are almost always very dangerous.

HAMMAM

The *hammam* is an eastern steam bath. In most stories it means a public bath, where men and women bathe separately.

KADI

The *kadi* is the judge in Islamic courts. Originally he was a scholar of law who was responsible for all legal matters on behalf of God's representative on Earth, the caliph. In fairy tales he is often called upon to resolve conflicts.

MERMAID

A female hybrid, half woman and half fish, that lives in the water. Generally, *mermaids* are said to be particularly beautiful.

RAMADAN

Ramadan is the month in which Muslims fast. It lasts for twenty-nine or thirty days, and ends with the Festival of the Breaking of the Fast. During Ramadan, Muslims are not allowed to eat or drink anything between sunrise and sunset. This is a time when many devote themselves completely to their faith, believing that it will bring them closer to God.

SULTAN

The absolute ruler or king. *Sultan* was the title given to the rulers of the Ottoman (Turkish) Empire, and is used in fairy tales as the equivalent of king.

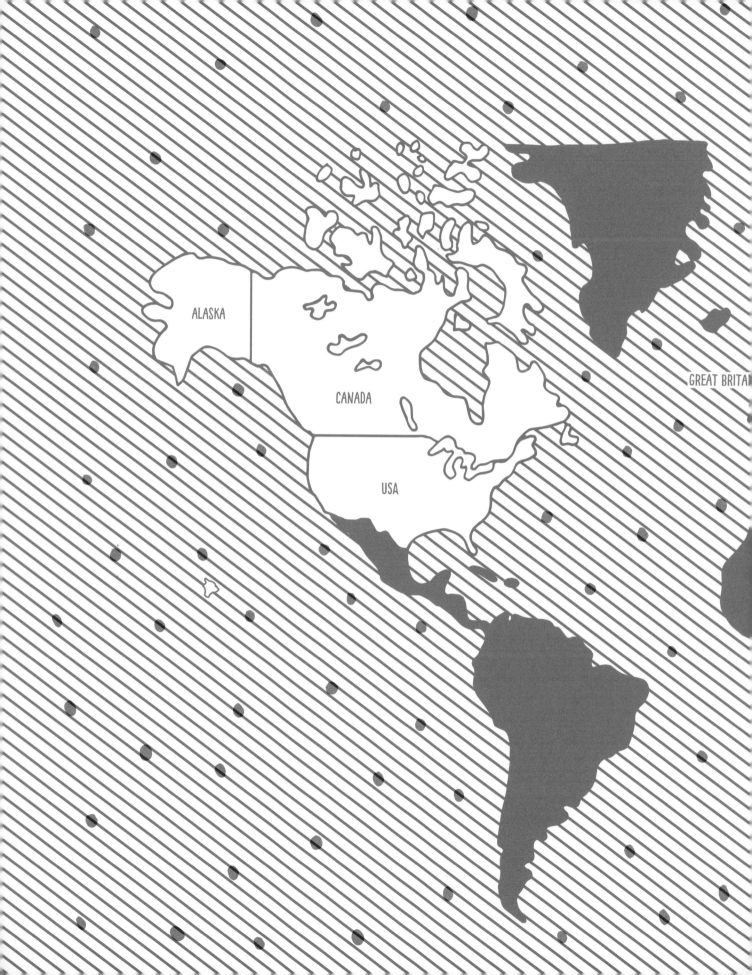

ALASKA

CANADA

USA

GREAT BRITAI

THE MIDDLE EAST

AUSTRALIA

NEW ZEALAND

◆ THE MIDDLE EAST AND THE FAR EAST OR ORIENT ◆

Nowadays when we talk of the "Middle East," we mean a part of Asia. The continent of Asia is huge, and so we distinguish between "middle" and "far." The "middle" section is closer to Europe, and the "far" comprises such countries as China and Japan.

Europe is also referred to as the "West," and we talk of "western culture." The "East" is seen from a European perspective and simply means what lies east of Europe. Not everyone agrees about which countries belong to the Middle East, but often those that are in the Arabian Peninsula and those of the "Fertile Crescent" are combined under that name. The "Arabian Peninsula" consists of Kuwait, Bahrain, Oman, Qatar, Saudi Arabia, The United Arab Emirates, and Yemen. The "Fertile Crescent" comprises Iraq, Syria, Lebanon, Israel, Palestine, and Jordan. Turkey is often included as well. It's called a crescent because the shape of the region is a bit like a half moon.

The climate in the Middle East is mainly hot and dry. Many people wear headscarves to protect themselves from the sun. However, the headscarf is also worn for traditional and religious reasons. Most people in the region are Muslims, which means that their religion is Islam. However, there are also Christian and Jewish communities in the Middle East.

Most of these countries speak Arabic, but Kurds speak Kurdish, most Iraqis speak Persian, and Hebrew is the national language of Israel.

WHERE DO OUR FAIRY TALES COME FROM?

Storytelling is one of the oldest human traditions. Many of the most familiar themes of fairy stories come originally from Muslim cultures, and only found their way to Europe later on.

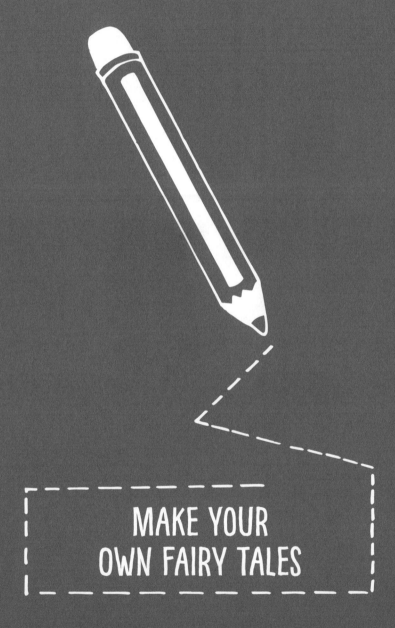

MAKE YOUR
OWN FAIRY TALES

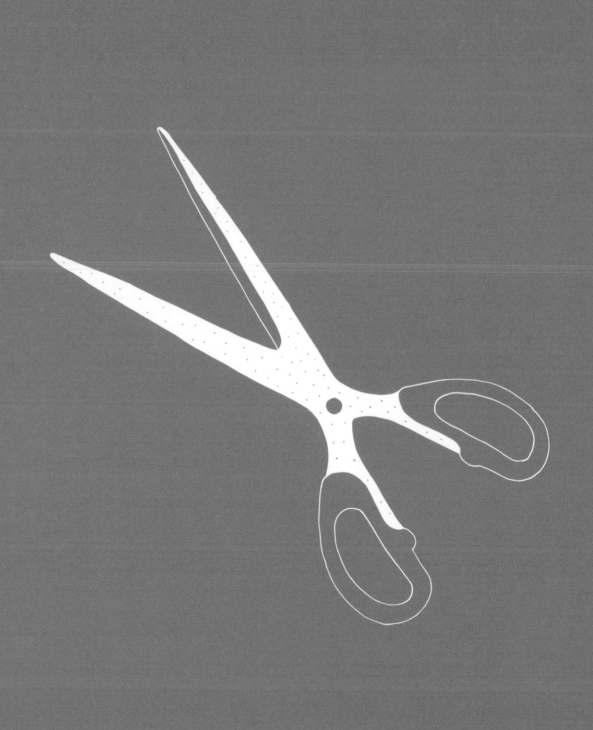

ENGLISH AND ARABIC SCRIPT

In English we write from left to right. The English alphabet with its twenty-six letters is derived from the Latin. This is the most widespread writing system in the world and is used in most European, African, and American countries. Every sound is symbolized by a letter.

Most alphabetical scripts used today originally stem from the so-called Phoenician script that came into use between the eleventh and fifth centuries BC. Both the Greek and the Aramaic scripts were derived from this, but they developed in different directions. Aramaic led to Arabic, and Greek to Latin, and hence to the alphabet we use today. Unlike Latin, Arabic consists solely of consonants (all the letters except A, E, I, O, and U). It is also written and read from right to left. The Arabic alphabet consists of twenty-eight letters instead of our own twenty-six, and most of these are linked together. Writing systems throughout the Islamic world are generally based on Arabic script. The next few pages offer you the chance to practice both languages, English and Arabic.

خ   خ

ر   ر

ا   ا

ف   ف

ه   ه

خرافة

FAIRY TALE

[xu'ra|fa]

[xu'] like the *ch* in the Scottish "och"

WOULD YOU LIKE TO TRY AND WRITE ARABIC?

As you have already learned, the Arabic alphabet is very complicated. Sounds are combined to form each word. Similarly shaped letters are separated from one another by additional points, and this is what gives words their different meanings. Accordingly, no matter whether an individual letter stands at the beginning, middle, or end of a word, it is either written in full or, occasionally, slightly shortened.

In the Arabic for "fairy tale," you can practice putting five letters together to form the whole word. Try it. But remember that you must write from right to left.

CH

Pronounced like the *ch* in the Scottish "och" | 7th letter in the alphabet | Like *Charuuf,* which means sheep.

RA

Pronounced as a rolled *R* [Scottish] | 10th letter in the alphabet | Like *Rijl,* which means leg.

ALIF

ا

Pronounced like *eh* | 1st letter in the alphabet | Like *Asad,* which means lion.

FA

Pronounced like *F* | 20th letter in the alphabet | Like *Farascha,* which means butterfly.

HA

Pronounced like *H* | 26th letter in the alphabet | Like *Hadiyya,* which means gift.

COMPLETE THE PATTERN

In Arab countries, most important buildings like mosques and palaces are decorated with brightly colored, patterned tiles. Put together, these often form a large and unified work of art. The patterns are often symmetrical and are therefore capable of unlimited extensions. See if you can complete this pattern.

FRANZISKA MEINERS was born in 1992 in Siegen, Germany. She studied communications design at the University of Applied Sciences in Aachen. Her interest is in the exchange of cultures and the role that media design can play in creating awareness and mutual understanding. This was the motivation behind her first children's book, *Whisper of the East*, which was her final dissertation. Franziska Meiners lives in Cologne, where she works as a freelance designer and illustrator.

THE END

A		B		C	
APPLE	تُفَّاحَةٌ	BIRD	طَائِرٌ	CAMEL	جَمَلٌ

G		H		I	
GOLD	ذَهَبٌ	HEART	قَلْبٌ	ISLAND	جَزِيرَةٌ

M		N		O	
MOON	قَمَرٌ	NOSE	أَنْفٌ	OASIS	يَنْبُوعٌ

S		T		U	
SUN	شَمْسٌ	TREE	شَجَرَةٌ	UMBRELLA	مِظَلَّةٌ

Y		Z	
PYRAMID	هَرَمٌ	ZEBRA	حِمَارٌ وَحْشِيٌّ